Splash!

Illustrations by

Ann Kronheimer

DEAN

I'm so excited my tummy feels funny. I got my first swimming badge last week, so I'm going swimming in the big pool today.

"What's that man going to do?" I ask.
"Judo, I think, says Dad. "There are lots of different sports to do here."

In the changing room, Mum helps me undo
my buttons, but I can do everything else myself.
I check to make sure my swimming
badge won't come off.

The locker key is on a pink rubber band.
Mum lets me put it on my wrist because
I'm going to the big pool.

Daniel can swim a little bit,
but best of all he likes to splash around
in the baby pool.

Dad climbs down into the water,
but I'm not sure I want to get in just yet.
"I can't see the bottom of the pool,"
I tell Dad.

"Will my feet touch the floor, Dad?" I ask.
"Of course they will,"
he tells me.

The water makes his legs look funny and I can't stop laughing. I wiggle my toes in the water and it feels nice.

Lots of other people are in the water having fun.
I want to get in too, now.

When Dad holds my hands I take my feet off the floor. I'm not so scared now.

The slide is the best thing at the big pool!

I hit the water with a

SplaSh!

Daniel wriggles around when Dad tries to dry him with a big, fluffy towel.

I'm almost dry now, but my socks are still sticking to my feet! Mum squeezes our costumes and they drip all over the floor.

"I want to go to the big pool," says Daniel.
"You will when you're big like me," I tell him.

Moving Day

Illustrations by

Ann Kronheimer

"Hurry up, Georgia! Come along, Daniel!
Today's a big day," says Gran.

Mum and Dad are too busy to sit down.
Our house looks strange and all our things are
in bags and boxes.

"Where are you taking our plant?" I ask.
"It's going to the new house," says the man.

"Where are you taking Dad's chair?"
I ask the other man.
"It's going to the new house too," he says.

Mum shows us our room. It's almost empty.
"Here are your special boxes for all your toys," she says.

Harvey Rabbit, Martin the Monkey, Minnie Miller ...
I make sure everything is there.
"I'm bringing Albert," says Daniel. "He's mine."

"Please don't lose my things," I say.
"Be nice to Joe," says Daniel.
"I'll be very careful," says the man.

The man says that everything is going in the
big van and nothing will get lost.

When we get to our new house,
I ask Dad where our things are.
"In your special boxes, of course," he says.
"They'll be in your new room."

"When are we going home?" asks Daniel.
"This is our home now," I tell him.
"Good! We've got stairs here," he grins.

Harvey Rabbit, Marvin the Monkey, Minnie Miller ...
Good! everything is still there.
Where shall I put my things in my very own room?

Daniel loves his new room.
"This is my new room, Albert," he says.

Best of all, we have a garden!
"I like slides, Georgia," grins Daniel.

"And I like our new house!" I say.

I like our new neighbour, too.
"More tea, Kim?"